To Deakie Boy and Rainey, Daddy John and Miss Mikey

9/26/01

To Margaret:

I Hope you enjoy
meeting my family!

Michele Y. Green

WILLIE PEARL:
UNDER THE MOUNTAIN

by Michelle Y. Green

Illustrations by Steve McCracken

William Ruth and Company

Published by William Ruth and Company
3202 Brinkley Road
Temple Hills, Maryland 20748

Printed in the United States of America.
First Edition.

Designed by Oliver W. Green, Jr.

Illustrations by Steve McCracken

ISBN 0-9627697-1-1

FOREWORD

Webster defines 'anticipate' as "to feel or know beforehand," and though we were filled with excitement and high hopes, we could not have know beforehand the warm and satisfying reception *Willie Pearl* would receive.

Willie Pearl was nominated for the Newbery Award and the Coretta Scott King Award, and was the recipient of numerous awards for writing and illustration. Adding to our pleasure was the acceptance of *Willie Pearl* to the core curriculum for the Compton Unified School District, a culturally diverse system in the Los Angeles area, thus making *Willie Pearl* required reading for fourth graders. Indeed, all of this recognition was gratifying. But real fulfillment came through the response of the readers, young and old alike. Again and again, they spoke of the anticipation they felt for the next installment in our series, *Willie Pearl: Under the Mountain.*

It is with pleasure that I announce the anticipation is over, and I know beforehand that you're in for a treat. Again, I thank you for your support, and I invite you to sit back, relax, and enjoy.

William E. Holmes
President
William Ruth and Company

Chapter 1

Springtime had come to the mountains, and the holler filled with life again. Ash trees, nubby with young leaves, covered the bare slopes. Wild violets, daffodils, and sweet williams made each front yard a patchwork. Squirrels and chipmunks played tag in the mushy soil, and tadpoles wriggled in the creek bottom.

From a screened upstairs window, Willie Pearl looked out over the freshly painted houses that lined the road of Number 6 holler. Cool mountain air, tinged with coal smoke, tickled her nose. Springtime was Willie Pearl's favorite time of year. She smiled, and sat, and looked.

"Willie . . . Willie Pearl," Ma Rainey's voice broke the spell. "If you don't get moving, you'll be late for school. And, you haven't even set out the wash water yet."

A tug of her woolen stockings, a twist of her dark braids, and Willie Pearl was down the stairs. She stopped at the bottom just long enough to lace up her brown hightops and grab for her hand-me-down coat.

"Morning, Ma," Willie Pearl said as she hurried through the kitchen on her way to the back porch. Ma Rainey was busy wiping a buttermilk mustache from little Clint's face with her apron.

"Button up that coat, young lady," insisted Ma Rainey without even turning around. "It's airish out there."

Ma Rainey seemed to know everything. Willie Pearl was convinced that her mother had an extra pair of eyes tucked

1

Chapter 1

away in the back of her head.

"Yes, ma'am," Willie Pearl said as she struggled to fasten the last coat button. She raised up just in time to see her brother Johnny stab the last fried pork chop on the breakfast table.

"You're gonna be late," taunted Susie Mae, "and you know Miss Wilson has been waiting to break in her new willow switches." Susie Mae was already wiping the breakfast dishes that Papa and the other miners had left earlier. Willie Pearl pretended not to hear her older sister. She banged out the back door, an empty lard bucket in each hand.

Every Monday was wash day at the Mahone house, and every Monday it was Willie Pearl's job to set out the wash water. Up and down, up and down—the water pump handle was frosty and cold to the touch. Not even a beautiful spring day was enough to coax the water out of the ground any faster. Willie Pearl pumped four or five times before the icy water gurgled into her pail.

Across the yard, two number 3 washtubs sat on a wooden bench, woefully empty. A third tub was already filled and sitting beside the bench on an old powder box.

"I'll never get finished in time," complained Willie Pearl out loud as she lugged the water back and forth across the yard. Because each bucket held only one gallon, it would take seven or eight trips to fill each tub. Fetching the wash water was hard work, but in the Mahone house, everyone was used to that. Wash day was no different.

Willie Pearl's older brother Johnny had gotten up early to gather the firewood and stack it under the big, black laundry pot. He had filled the pot with water and set it to boil.

Little brother Clint had set out the homemade cakes of lye soap and the blueing for the final rinse. He also had to make

2

sure that Ma's rub board, clothespins, and wooden chunking stick were at the ready.

Susie Mae, who liked to sleep in late, had sorted the dirty laundry the night before. The first pile was for kitchen towels, tablecloths, and "dainties" as Ma called them. Next came the everyday clothes—the few school shirts and overalls for the boys, and the two or three cotton dresses for Susie Mae and Willie Pearl. Then came the sweaty, dusty muckers that the men wore into the mine. Susie Mae had been careful to pick up each of these pieces gingerly so as not to get any of the gritty coal dust on her own clothes.

Susie Mae also had to check each piece for loose buttons or tiny holes for mending. She and Willie Pearl only had a few dresses apiece, which had to last until Ma Rainey made new ones next Christmas. The boys' overalls were store-bought, and of course, the men got their work clothes from the Consolidated Coal Company. The coal company owned Number 6 mine where Papa and the rest of the men worked, and it owned the Company Store where all the families traded for goods.

"One more trip should do it!" Willie Pearl trudged back to the water pump. The amount of mud on her boots let her know that she had not done such a good job of keeping all of the water in the buckets. The bottom half of her coat was wet through. She sat the buckets down beside the pump to catch her breath, then filled them for what she hoped was the last time.

Just at that moment, a high-pitched screech stole Willie Pearl's attention. Two blue jays were fighting over some scraps of biscuit and the few rinds of fatback that Ma had put out. Willie Pearl stopped in her tracks to watch, full buckets in hand. The birds circled and swooped and pecked angrily at each other's backs. They dove, and turned, and chased each other across the yard. Seeing the birds fight over the scraps reminded Willie Pearl that she had not taken time for breakfast. Her stomach growled a loud, long reminder.

"Hey, why are you just standing there, Willie Pearl?" chided an impatient voice from the back door.

Sploosh! Two full buckets of icy, cold water hit the ground at the same time. It was Willie Pearl's best friend, Mae Ella.

"Mae Ella, you liked to scare the daylights out of me," answered Willie Pearl. "How long have you been at the door?"

"Long enough to see that you're going to be late again," Mae Ella fussed. "The others have left for school already. We'll have to run all the way there."

"Why don't you grab one of these buckets and help me?" Willie Pearl asked. She dabbed hopelessly at the big wet patch in the front of her coat with a balled up pocket handkerchief.

"No sense both of us getting wet up. Besides, that doesn't look like any fun at all." Mae Ella stood fast and munched on one of Ma's biscuits.

"It's not supposed to be fun . . . don't you fetch water for Miss Vera?" Willie Pearl sloshed yet another bucket into the wash tub.

"Me? Fetch water? Why should I? You don't think Aunt Vera does her own laundry, do you?" Mae Ella brushed the biscuit crumbs from the front of her new spring coat.

Even though the two ten-year-old girls were best friends, Willie Pearl couldn't help but feel a little jealous. Mae Ella had it made. She was an only child living with her maiden aunt. It was no secret that Mae Ella was more than a little spoiled. Most of the other kids in the camp didn't like her at all. But

*Sploosh! Two full buckets of icy, cold water
hit the ground at the same time.*

Chapter 1

Willie Pearl thought everyone deserved a best friend—and Willie Pearl was determined to be it.

"I'm done now," sighed Willie Pearl at last. "Let's go." She grabbed the two buckets and hoped she could make it back through the house before Ma Rainey could notice her soggy coat.

Mae Ella tracked in behind her friend. Willie Pearl sat the buckets on the back porch and called out a hasty good-bye to her mother. A quick glance at the breakfast table told Willie Pearl what she already had feared. Mae Ella had helped herself to the very last biscuit.

"Just a minute young lady. One thing before you go," called out Ma Rainey from the front room.

"Ma must have two sets of eyes," Willie Pearl thought to herself. "And both pair can see through walls." Willie Pearl clutched at the front of her coat and edged toward the doorway of the front room. Ma Rainey drew near and smoothed her daughter's long black braids.

"Next wash day, spend *less* time daydreaming and *more* time being on time for school," her mother said. Then, looking down she added, "and try a little harder to get at least some water *in* the buckets." Ma shook Willie Pearl's braids back and forth playfully and kissed her daughter quickly on the forehead.

"One more thing," Ma Rainey said, reaching into her apron pocket. "I thought you might have just enough time to finish one of these."

Willie Pearl opened the small bundle wrapped in butcher paper to find one of Ma's wonderful biscuits. A generous layer of sweet, dark molasses oozed out the sides.

"Now scoot, both of you," Ma teased.

Willie Pearl chomped one enormous bite then bounded

down the steep front steps two at a time. Mae Ella struggled to keep up. Moments later, both girls slid into their seats just as Miss Wilson's bell sounded its last clang. It was a fine spring morning, after all.

Chapter 2

Saturday morning couldn't come fast enough for Willie Pearl. After weeks and weeks of waiting, she would not be put off any longer. Johnny had to keep his promise today—or else. But first, there were chores to do.

In the coal camps, a layer of gritty, black soot settled on everything. It was Willie Pearl's job to keep the front porch, stone steps, and the boardwalk to their neighbor's house swept clean. During the week, a "once over" with the corn broom was enough. But on Saturdays, nothing less than a full scrubbing would do.

"Make sure it's clean enough for the Preacher to eat Sunday dinner off of," insisted Ma Rainey. Reverend Webb seemed to find his way up to the Mahone house for Sunday chicken and dumplings more times than not. Papa joked that the only thing left when Reverend Webb finished eating Ma's "gospel bird" was the feet and the beak.

Willie Pearl struck the floor boards again and again with the corn broom. Clouds of coal dust flew. Next, she plunged the broom into a waiting pail of hot, soapy water. Billows of suds covered the front porch and the tops of her brown boots. Nearly done, Willie Pearl's excitement rose like the soap bubbles that drifted beyond the porch front.

Johnny was busy laying in coal from the coal shed out back. Tomorrow was Sunday, so he had to be sure there would be enough to keep the coal stove going for two days. There was lump coal for the cook stove in the kitchen, and slack coal to bank the fire in the front room. Chunk after chunk of the precious black ore tumbled into the coal scuttle.

From the front porch, Willie Pearl strained to hear the sound of Johnny's shovel scraping across the coal house floor. As long as she heard him working, Willie Pearl knew Johnny was still around. She couldn't take the chance that he might forget—or worse—slip off on purpose.

"Yoo-hoo, *illie-Way earl-Pay*. . .Would you like to come over and *lay-pay ith-way e-may?*" Mae Ella's pig latin was terrible, but good enough for Willie Pearl to understand that Mae Ella was inviting her over to play. *illie-Way earl-Pay* yelled back to the porch several houses away.

"Not today, Mae Ella . . . I mean *ae-May lla-Eay*." Mae Ella's name was nearly impossible to pronounce in pig latin. "*Ot-nay oday-tay*—not today." Then, feeling she owed her best friend some kind of explanation, Willie Pearl added, "too much work." A twinge of guilt hit Willie Pearl. She hadn't meant to lie, especially to her best friend. "I just want her to be surprised when she sees what I've got," Willie Pearl said to herself, figuring that was a good enough reason. Willie Pearl tried her best to get back to work, but Mae Ella was not going to give up so easily.

"I thought we could walk down to Jenkins Theatre and catch the new Hoot Gibson feature," Mae Ella persisted. "Aunt Vera gave me 11 cents for my ticket."

Willie Pearl stopped working and leaned on her soapy broom. "It's not every day that a new Hoot Gibson feature comes to town," she thought. "And maybe I could borrow some of the money from Johnny . . . ." But thinking of Johnny only reminded her of her own important plans.

"No, thank you just the same," Willie Pearl decided with a

firm swish of her broom.

"I'll let you hold my popcorn . . . ." Mae Ella was one girl who was used to getting her own way. But on this day, she was no match for Willie Pearl.

"Maybe next time," came the determined reply. The front door to Miss Vera's slammed hard enough to be heard clear across the holler, and Mae Ella stomped inside.

Willie Pearl tossed the rest of the soapy water across the porch, then ran out back to get the rinse water. It was only then she noticed—the door to the coal shed was latched tight. Johnny was nowhere to be found.

"Darn that Mae Ella!" Willie Pearl was quick to blame her friend. "Thanks to you, Johnny got away."

Willie Pearl craned her neck down the road just in time to see Johnny disappear around the bend. And he was not alone. Four or five boys had joined him, kicking up stones as they went.

Willie Pearl quickly filled her bucket with rinse water. "If I hurry, I can still catch him before he gets away."

Willie Pearl rushed to complete her task. With a final swirl of suds, Willie Pearl was down the road, tracking behind her brother and his friends.

Chapter 3

"Brice, you be the lookout!" one of the older boys yelled. "Remember the signals—one long hoot as soon as you see someone come 'round the bend, two short hoots if it's a grown up."

The opening to Number 6 mine was just a stone's throw across the road from the holler. Years before, the Consolidated Coal Company had blasted its way into the side of the mountain. The mine entrance gaped open like a wide, dark mouth.

Brice scrambled on top of the sand house and perched down low. He hated being the one who lost the draw. Worse still was being posted as lookout and missing all the fun below. He took out a stack of well-worn bubble gum cards from his back pocket and began flipping through them to pass the time. The rest of the boys snuck into the sand house, ready for some big fun.

The sand house was a large shed near the entrance of the mine. Inside were mounds and mounds of fine, warm sand kept dry by electric lights. The miners sprinkled sand on the railway tracks when the coal cars had to pull uphill. The sand kept the metal wheels from slipping. On workdays, the sand house was busy. But on Saturdays, it made a perfect secret meeting place.

"Let's see who's gonna be the sandman this time," announced A.C. He was kin to the Mahones and the ringleader of the group. Each boy dug into his pocket and pulled out his lucky shooter marble. A.C. drew a circle in the sand and stepped way back. "Okay," he said, drawing a line with his foot. "I'll shoot

Chapter 3

first, then you, then you, then you."

Even though Johnny was the second oldest in the group, he was short for his age. It made the other boys treat him years younger. A.C. knelt down on one knee, squinted one eye, and readied the marble between his thumb and index finger.

"Fo-o-o-o-sh—out popped the marble in a fast, straight line. It left a faint trail in the sand as it entered the circle and stopped just before the far edge.

"Good shot," said Floyd. "Me next." One by one, each boy took his turn until finally, it was Johnny's chance to shoot.

"Too much," said A.C. "Looks like you're it!"

In an instant, the four boys piled on Johnny and held him down on the sandy floor. Two grabbed his ankles and began winding rope around each of his pant legs. Johnny hollered loudly, half laughing, half trying to get free. Out of the corner of his eye, he saw A.C. lugging a bucket of sand from across the shed.

James and Buster hoisted Johnny to his feet and popped the braces on his bib overalls. Kicking and yelling did no good as A.C. began pouring the scratchy sand down the front of Johnny's overalls. Johnny could feel the heaviness in his legs. The empty space between his long underwear and denim overalls filled with sand. When the job was done, the boys took off, chanting "Run, run, fast as you can, but you can't catch me, you old Mr. Sandman."

Johnny tried to chase behind the boys, growling in a monster's voice. But walking in the heavy pants was very difficult. Four or five steps were all he could manage before he fell to the sand house floor. Johnny flapped his arms wildly and tried to lift his sand-filled legs. Try as he might, he could not get up.

Willie Pearl: Under the Mountain

*The empty space between his long underwear
and denim overalls filled with sand.*

Chapter 3

Everyone laughed until they doubled over. Everyone, that is, except Johnny, who could not move. They were laughing so hard that they didn't hear Brice's signal at first. By the time they did, it was too late.

"Let go of my brother!" demanded a girl's voice angrily. It was Willie Pearl. She charged at one of the boys and began pounding him with her clenched fists.

"I couldn't help it," stammered Brice. "She just snuck up on me," he explained, bubble gum cards still in hand.

"It's alright, Willie Pearl," said Johnny between laughs. "I don't need your help. It's just a game." Buster and Floyd helped Johnny to his feet and began untying his ankles.

"What are you doing here anyway?" A.C. demanded. "This place is off limits to girls!"

It was true. The mine was strictly off limits to anyone who did not work there, but especially to females. The miners believed that women brought bad luck to the mines, so they weren't allowed anywhere near.

"I sorta followed you here," Willie Pearl confessed slowly. "I wanted to see what you were up to."

"Promise you won't tell, and we won't tell your Pa that you jinxed the mine," A.C. threatened. The other boys circled around her in a tight clump.

"I didn't jinx anything," said Willie Pearl. "I was just trying to find my brother."

"Lay off her, fellas," said Johnny, who was shaking out the rest of the sand from his pant legs. "She's alright. We can trust her."

"When I saw you going down the hill, I thought you had forgotten all about . . . you know . . . your promise." Willie Pearl cut her eyes at the other boys standing around. She hoped that

14

Johnny wouldn't give it away.

"Promise?" Johnny stopped for a moment. "Oh, that. Don't worry, there's plenty of time."

"But can't we go right now? It's already past noon," Willie Pearl begged. Everyone was looking at Johnny for his answer.

"You sure you're ready for this, sis?" he asked one last time.

Willie Pearl would never admit that she was just the tiniest bit afraid, especially in front of Johnny's friends. She bent down and picked up Johnny's lucky shooter marble where it lay in the sand. "Let's go now!" Willie Pearl exclaimed. "I can't wait another minute."

Chapter 4

Willie Pearl ran all the way home ahead of Johnny. "If we hurry," she told herself, "I bet I could be the best in the holler before supper time."

Willie Pearl scrambled up the hill beside the stone steps. The steps gleamed white from their recent scrubbing, and Willie Pearl did not want to mess them up. She balanced along the edge of the boardwalk, then the front porch, and entered the house. Willie Pearl walked briskly through the front room and breezed through the kitchen on her way to the back porch.

"Where to in such a hurry, miss?" asked Ma. Ma was busy pounding out a piece of cube steak for Saturday night's supper. Besides the evening meal, most of the cooking for Sunday dinner had to be done on Saturdays, too. There were green beans to snap, chicken feathers to pluck, cornbread dressing to fix, and sweet potato pies yet to bake. Willie Pearl paused just long enough to eye a pan of rolls on the rise.

"Me and Johnny are working on a project," Willie Pearl answered. "It's a surprise."

"Johnny and I," corrected Ma Rainey. "And don't bang that door!"

"Johnny and I," repeated Willie Pearl heading back out through the kitchen. She carried with her a short-handled axe.

"Before you take off, I need you to run down to the Company Store," said Ma. "Get me 15 cents worth of salt pork, and tell Mr. Fletcher to put it on Papa's account."

Willie Pearl glanced out the kitchen window. Johnny was still waiting for her at the bottom of the steps. She had already lost sight of him once today, and she wanted to make sure it didn't happen again.

"Yes, ma'am," answered Willie Pearl half-heartedly. Ma Rainey could not help but notice the anxious look on her daughter's face.

"You know," Ma said suddenly, "I'll bet Susie Mae would run to the store for you if you did the washing up tonight."

Willie Pearl found her twelve-year-old sister out in the hen house trying to chase down an old biddy.

"You'll sing a different tune tomorrow when you're covered up with gravy," Susie yelled above the squawking. It occurred to Willie Pearl that this was not the best time to ask for any favors. But, ready or not, she had to take that chance.

"Well, alright," Susie Mae said. "But you have to do the Sunday washing up for me as well."

Saturday night dishes were bad enough, but Sunday dishes were even worse. It was a bad deal, but Willie Pearl was in no mood to argue. "Thanks," offered Willie Pearl, turning to go. At last, nothing else stood in the way.

"Over here, sis!" Johnny answered his sister's call. He had gone up the road a piece and was hurling stones into the ditch.

"C'mon," Willie Pearl said gleefully. "I'm ready for my very own pair of stilts."

Willie Pearl had started pestering her brother to make her some stilts at the first sign that winter was over. Week after week, Johnny had insisted, "It's still too muddy. We'll have to wait." But today, the ground was firm, the chores were done, and there was still plenty of daylight left. Willie Pearl could hardly believe the day had finally come.

Chapter 4

"What's wrong with tom walkers, anyway?" Johnny asked heading up the gravel road.

"Tom walkers are fun, alright," Willie Pearl admitted, "but I want to be as tall as the trees!"

Willie Pearl remembered the tom walkers that she and Mae Ella made last spring. Each of them had saved two number 8 cans of evaporated milk and soaked off the labels. Johnny had helped them punch two holes on either side and string the cans with a loop of shot wire. Clip clop, clip clop. With a tom walker on each foot, Willie Pearl could pretend that she was a noble princess atop a fine white stallion. But that was nothing to compare to the fun she could imagine with her own pair of stilts.

"This way," said Johnny making a sudden turn off the path. Johnny took off up the hill beyond old lady Chinkapin's house, hatchet in hand. Johnny sprung up the hill like a young jack rabbit, but then he didn't have to stop to hitch up his long, black stockings every few steps. Willie Pearl tried her best to keep up with him. Out of breath, and with one slightly skinned knee, Willie Pearl finally met up with him in a grove of young ash trees.

"Make them tall as you can," Willie Pearl insisted. "I want to look out over the whole holler . . . the whole world!" She stood on tip toe and raised her arms high overhead.

"Hold on a minute, Butch," protested Johnny. "If I make them too tall, you'll never be able to get on them. And that makes them double hard to walk on, too."

Johnny should know. Johnny was the best stilt-maker in the whole holler. And he was the reigning stilt-walking champion. The church picnic last spring had proved that. Johnny wasn't the tallest boy in his class, but when it came to

Willie Pearl: Under the Mountain

*"I want to look out over the whole
holler . . . the whole world!"*

19

stilt-walking, not even A.C. could beat him.

"This one looks good." Johnny's expert eye fell upon a straight young sapling about six-feet high. Most important, it had a sturdy joint about eighteen inches up.

"Here, wrap your fingers around this one to see how it fits," said Johnny. He watched as Willie Pearl closed her fingers around the young tree.

"Perfect," he said. "That will give you a good grip. Now, rest your foot right about here."

With a little help, Willie Pearl raised one foot to the joint in the tree. It fit comfortably beneath her muddy leather boot.

"This'll do just fine," Johnny confirmed. A few swift chops of the hatchet, and down it fell.

"I want to be as good a stilt-walker as you. Will you teach me?" Willie Pearl asked her brother.

"There's really nothing to it, sis," Johnny assured her. "You just put one foot in front of the other." Johnny trimmed off the leaves and switches with the hatchet.

"Aren't you afraid of falling down?" she asked. Willie Pearl rubbed her knee, which had begun to sting a bit.

"You can't look at it that way, or you'd never try anything," Johnny answered matter-of-factly. "Sure, it's a little scary at first, but if you keep putting one foot in front of the other, you'll get through!" Johnny propped the fallen tree against an old rotting log.

"Now for the other one," he said. "While I'm looking for another tree, why don't you strip off the bark and make it nice and smooth." Johnny dug into one of the pockets of his denim overalls and handed Willie Pearl a small pocket knife. It was shiny new and red.

"Be careful now," Johnny warned. "It's brand new and extra

sharp. I wouldn't want you to get hurt."

"Where'd you get this?" Willie Pearl asked, turning it over and over in her hand.

"It took me three weeks of hauling coal to make enough to get this," Johnny said. His chest stuck out just a bit. "Isn't it a beauty?"

Johnny made spending money by delivering coal to some of the neighbors up and down the holler. Most of the time, families bought coal from the coal man when he came around. But, sometimes they made do with the low-grade coal that fell alongside the railroad tracks or tumbled from the coal tipple. Johnny gathered the free coal in old potato sacks or onion bags and sold it for 10 cents a load.

Willie Pearl slowly unfolded the blade. She felt proud that her older brother trusted her with something so precious. It was special enough that he was letting her help make the stilts. But now he was even letting her use his brand new pocket knife. She liked the way that Johnny always made her feel important—even when his buddies were around. Thanks to Johnny, Willie Pearl could skip a rock, shimmy up a tree, and play "jump the ditch" with the best of them.

Willie Pearl took her time and stripped the bark from the sapling with precision. When she finished, she carved the letters "W.P." into the wood right where the joints met. "I'll put a letter 'J' on the other one," she told herself. She couldn't wait to show Johnny her handiwork.

What was that? Willie Pearl heard a strange noise that seemed to come from several yards away. "Johnny, is that you?" Willie Pearl called out, suddenly afraid. "Johnny?"

Willie Pearl peered through the leafy grove and saw no signs of her brother. She took a few cautious steps in front of her, toward the muffled sound.

"Johnny, stop fooling around now. Is that you?" Willie Pearl held her stilt in front of her, as if to ward off some unknown enemy.

"Sh-h-h-h! Come here, quick!" came a familiar reply. Timidly, Willie Pearl advanced a few more steps. She could *hear* her brother, but she couldn't see him.

"Where are you?" she called again.

"Down here." There, a few yards away, was Johnny standing shoulder deep in a crack in the surface of the mountain. The trench was as wide as the creek that ran at the bottom of Number 6 holler, but there was no water in it—only lots of rotting leaves and dead branches.

"Strange noises," he said, still whispering. "I can't tell what."

"Noises?" Willie Pearl gasped. Every boogey man and haint that Willie Pearl had ever imagined flashed into mind.

"Ghosts?" she asked aloud.

"No, sis. Listen!" I think they're coming from the mine. Come here." Johnny gave his sister a hand-down into the trench. He used Willie Pearl's newly cut stilt to support himself.

"Hold onto this." Johnny gestured to a gnarled tree root. Slowly, carefully, Willie Pearl descended into the crack and scootched down near her brother. She cupped her free hand to her ear and strained to listen.

Johnny was right! Willie Pearl couldn't make out the sounds clearly, but there was no doubt that they were coming from far down below.

"But what could it be?" Willie Pearl asked. "Nobody works the mine on Saturday. And there was no one there just a few hours ago."

"You're right," Johnny admitted. "But, I don't get it. If it's not miners, what then?"

Willie Pearl was short on courage, but long on imagination. "Whatever it is, I'm not sticking around here to find out," she said. "Let's get out of here—quick!" Willie Pearl scrambled out on all fours, not waiting for Johnny's help.

"We'd better tell Papa about this," she said when she finally reached the top. The front of her dress was smudged with grass and mud, and one stocking had popped its garter.

"No, let's not tell a soul," Johnny said, pulling himself out with the help of the pole. "No one has to know. Not yet, anyway. We'll get to the bottom of this, and then surprise everyone. It'll be our special secret."

If there was anything Willie Pearl liked more than a good secret, it was being the first one to solve a mystery. But this was different. This was scary!

"You're not an old scaredy cat, are you?" It was as if Johnny could read her mind.

Willie Pearl hesitated. Would Johnny still help her learn to stilt-walk if she didn't go in on this? And wouldn't Mae Ella and the others be impressed when they sprung the news!

"Okay," she agreed finally. "It'll be just between us."

"Great! Now grab onto this. I want to see how it fits." Johnny handed her the long pole. It was a perfect fit.

"You can finish the trimming later," he said. "For now, let's see how they work together. I'll give you a leg-up."

Willie Pearl gripped the pole tightly, took a deep breath, and placed her right foot on one stilt. Then, clutching Johnny's shoulder, she sprung atop the other stilt. A wiggle, a wobble, and Willie Pearl stood up straight for a few seconds before falling forward.

Chapter 4

"Try it again," Johnny reassured her. "You can't just stand still. You gotta move to keep from falling." Willie Pearl could see that this wasn't going to be as easy as she thought. In fact, she was starting to think that tom walkers weren't so bad after all.

Johnny handed her the stilts again. "Don't give up," he said firmly. "Remember, it all depends on you. Just put one foot in front of the other until you're through."

Chapter 5

Sunday came and went at the Mahone house pretty much as usual. There was Sunday school, then church, and then a B.Y.P.U. meeting to discuss the upcoming Spring bazaar. As expected, Reverend Webb found a reason to drop in just about time for Sunday supper. When he finally finished eating, there was just time enough to do the washing up so as not to be late for the evening church service.

Come Monday, Willie Pearl could barely keep her mind on her lessons. While everyone else was concentrating on their times tables, Willie Pearl was thinking about finishing her other stilt.

"Once I strip off the bark, I'm sure I'll keep my balance much better," she assured herself.

Willie Pearl was the first one out the door when class was over. There was no point in waiting for Mae Ella. Mae Ella was still pouting from Saturday. She barely spoke at recess and sat with Lulabelle Mosely at lunch. Most of all, she hadn't bothered inviting Willie Pearl to join her on the way home. Each week, Mae Ella liked to stop past the Company Store to buy a sackful of penny candies. She even shared some of them with her best friend, now and then.

Willie Pearl ran all the way home without stopping. She banged in the front door and flung her homemade book bag in one corner of the room. Even though it was only a little after three o'clock, the sun set fast in the mountains. The men would be coming in from the mine any time now, and supper was almost ready. Willie Pearl would have to hurry if she was going to have time to practice.

Johnny had waited until Saturday evening to lug the stilts to their hiding place beneath the porch. Willie Pearl didn't want anyone to know about them until she could stride with confidence for everyone to see. She pulled the unfinished stilt out and balanced it across her lap. The bark felt rough and sticky as she ran her hand back and forth across its length.

"Johnny will be so proud of me, especially when I show him where I carved his initials." It was then that Willie Pearl realized what she had not noticed before.

"The knife—what did I do with Johnny's knife?" In a panic, Willie Pearl sprang to her feet. She began searching frantically everywhere she could think of—under the porch, around the house, in her room. "Where could it be?"

Willie Pearl remembered her muddy, grass-stained dress. But it was already hanging on the clothesline out back. She shook the pockets anyway, hoping in vain that the precious item would be there.

"Did I give it back to him? When was the last time I had it?" A terrible dread came upon her as she thought back to Saturday afternoon. "I was using the knife when Johnny called me to come see the trench." Her stomach bunched up inside. "Could I have dropped it in the woods?" Willie Pearl knew the answer to that question lay among the ash trees.

"It was brand new. He'll be so mad at me," she moaned. "I can't let Johnny know. I'll have to go alone." The thought of visiting that spooky place alone was too awful to imagine. But the thought of disappointing her brother was far more terrible. "I've got to find it before he realizes it's missing," she said. "I'd better go right now."

"Willie Pearl, it's your turn to set the table," Ma called from the kitchen. Willie Pearl came inside and tried hard to forget about the awful feeling in her stomach. Each knife and fork she placed on the table only reminded her of her carelessness. Ma could tell right away that something was wrong.

"Everything go alright today at school?" she asked.

"Yes, ma'am," answered Willie Pearl. She didn't feel much like talking.

Ma waited a few minutes then said, "Haven't seen Mae Ella around for a few days. Did you two have another fight?"

"No, ma'am, I've just been a little busy. That's all," Willie Pearl squeezed out another answer. Ma tried again.

"How's that secret project coming along?" she asked her daughter cheerily.

"Oh fine," Willie Pearl answered. Then quickly, trying to change the subject, she added, "What's taking Papa so long? He's usually home by now."

This time it was Ma's turn to worry. She glanced up at the kitchen clock. Usually by the time the table was set, the men came bustling through the door. Five o'clock passed, and the sun was barely a sliver above the mountain. Six o'clock came. The men were more than an hour late.

Willie Pearl put aside her own troubles and started to sense that something even more important than Johnny's knife was at stake. Johnny, Susie Mae, and Clint hung around the front room, expecting to be called to supper at any time.

Ma waited for a while longer, but as the time passed, she told her children to come on to the table. Supper was eaten in silence. Even little Clint knew that this was no time for careless talk.

After supper, Willie Pearl, Susie Mae, and Johnny finished

Chapter 5

their book work and all their evening chores while they waited. Clint pressed his young face against the front room window, waiting for some sign of Papa, Mr. Lucias, and Mr. Jack. Ma kept the men's supper warming on the stove and busied herself in the kitchen. Bedtime drew near, and still no word came.

One last look out the window, and then . . . "They're coming, they're coming!" yelled Clint.

Ma's face changed instantly at Clint's news. She quickly checked her hair in the window glass and pinned in the few stray strands into a neat bun. The children crowded around the front door. At last, the three tired men came lumbering in.

"More rock fall today. I tell you, it ain't safe," grumbled Mr. Jack. He was talking fast and seemed angry.

"The foreman said he's got a crew coming in to check it out," Papa said. " 'Till then, there's nothing we can do."

Willie Pearl liked how Papa always seemed calm, even when danger was around. It made her feel safe. Papa set down his tools and headed straight for the supper table. He patted each of his children on the head as he strode through the front room.

"What's to check out?" continued Mr. Jack. "When you work the mines long enough, you don't need any big shots to tell you what you already know." Mr. Jack followed Papa into the kitchen, talking all the while.

"Any day now, there's gonna be trouble. This morning when we came in, those timbers were snapped in two like matchsticks. You could hear that roof just working. It's time to pull out of that vein, now," Mr. Jack insisted. "Why, even a one-eyed mule knows that." Mr. Jack plunked down into the worn cane-bottom chair so hard that Willie Pearl was afraid it would give way.

28

"Evening, Ol' Miss," Mr. Lucias spoke to Ma Rainey. He pulled up a seat to the table. Mr. Lucias was a newcomer to the mine. It was only last fall that he had left his family down south to come to Jenkins to work. Although he was a good worker, he was still just learning the ways of the mine.

"What happens if they find we're too close to the surface?" he asked.

"If they find it's not safe," said Papa tying his napkin around his neck, "they'll pull up the track and quit that section. Then, they'll blast it shut to keep it from caving in and hurting someone."

"That's what they should'a done last spring before poor old Andy got trapped," broke in Mr. Jack.

"What do you mean?" asked Mr. Lucias.

"They hemmed and hawed for days before they decided to blast it shut. Finally, it was too late. When the cave in started, Andy couldn't make it out in time. And leaving all those children, too, God bless 'em. I was there when they finally hauled his body out. Why I . . . ."

"That's enough," said Ma. "Little ears don't need to be hearing all this. Let's bless the table."

Conversation stopped, and the heads of the three men bowed over their weighted-down plates.

"Amen," added Ma Rainey with emphasis. "And thank you for bringing the men home safe one more time."

Papa looked up from his plate to find four heads crowding the kitchen doorway.

"I see we've got an audience tonight, Mahone," said Mr. Jack. "Why, Butch's eyes are big as signal lights." Willie Pearl flinched at the sound of her tomboy name.

"Why so late tonight, Papa?" asked Willie Pearl.

Chapter 5

"Six east place had rock fall just before quitting time," explained Papa. "We had to clean it out and shore it up so the engineers can take a look around. They've shut us down until then."

The Consolidated Coal Company ran three shifts at Number 6 mine. Papa's shift went in at daybreak and usually quit just before the sun slipped behind the mountain. The next shift worked from late afternoon until midnight, and the "Hoot Owl" shift worked until the sun came up the next day.

Each crew had a certain job to do. The first ones in were the trackmen. They laid down steel rails on the floor of the mine so the coal cars could run in and out. Then, they strung overhead wires for power. Next, came the timber men. Their job was to prop up the roof of the mine with large wooden posts to keep it from caving in. Last, the cutting machine was rolled in. A large motorized blade would slice into the face of the coal to prepare it for blasting.

Usually, the evening shifts laid the timber and track and cut the coal for the morning shift. But when there was rock fall, nobody left the mine until it was cleaned up and made safe for the next crew.

"How soon do you expect the safety inspectors in?" asked Mr. Lucias.

"They're bringing in a special team from Fairmont, West Virginia, so I suspect they'll be here in a day or two," reasoned Papa.

"Where do they think we'll tunnel out?" asked Mr. Lucias. He was already on his third helping of rice.

"Not sure yet, it could be almost anywhere, the way those tunnels twist and turn," answered Papa, reaching for another biscuit.

"All that rock fall, and the way that roof was shuddering and groaning . . . we could come up right in the middle of this kitchen table," said Mr. Jack.

Willie Pearl cut her eyes at Johnny. "So that's it!" she thought to herself. "That's why we heard those strange noises. They *were* coming from inside the mine! The men must be tunneling out near old lady Chinkapin's place." She could tell from Johnny's face that he was thinking the same thing. Still, a promise was a promise, and Willie Pearl wasn't going to be the one to blurt out anything.

"Until we know what's what, there's no sense in you kids fooling around up in those woods," Papa said sternly. His steel-grey eyes met those of his children. "Stay away from up there for the time being."

Papa had spoken. A half-hearted chorus of "Yes, Papa," met his ears. The four children knew that whether Papa was there or not, Ma Rainey's willow switches had a way of backing up Papa's orders.

"Susie Mae, Johnny, you help clear the table and help me wash up. Willie Pearl, see that Clint gets tucked into bed right away." If Papa was the head of the house, Ma was the arms, legs, and feet. She knew how to get the best out of everyone under her roof.

Willie Pearl went first up the dark staircase to light the room that she shared with her brothers and sister. She knew every bump and turn in the dark room by heart.

"Stay away from up there." Papa's words echoed in Willie Pearl's ears as she reached for the pull chain. "As soon as I fetch Johnny's knife, I will," she promised.

Chapter 6

Willie Pearl waited to leave until she heard the soft, easy breathing of her sister who slept beside her. In the dark, she pulled on her black stockings, slipped into her dress, and laced her boots up tight. Johnny stirred a bit on the other side of the divider curtain, but he did not wake up. Past her parents' room, down the steps, and out the door—Willie Pearl stepped into the night air.

The moon rose full and bright over the top of the mountain. The stars were so big and close, they seemed to hug the very ground. Willie Pearl took with her a red kerosene lamp to light the way, a box of matchsticks from the fireplace, and her one finished stilt. For some reason the stilt made her feel safe. And it was useful in her climb up the hill from old lady Chinkapin's house. Deep shadows criss-crossed the grass at sharp angles.

"First, I'll look around that old log where I was sitting," she said, talking to herself. "Why, I'll be back before Susie Mae turns over again." The ground beneath her boots was chilly and damp.

Just ahead was the ash grove where Johnny had picked out the choice sapling. Not far from there was the log where he had propped the fallen tree for Willie Pearl. The sky was nearly bright enough that she almost didn't need the lamp. She stooped way down and searched every inch of the log, on top and beneath. Then, she poked around the ground with her trusty stilt.

"It's just got to be here," she heard herself say. Willie Pearl sat down awhile on the log and rested the long pole beside her. She thought of how exciting Saturday had been. "If only I had been more careful," she said. Against her will, she felt tears start to fall. "Oh, Johnny, I didn't mean to lose your knife. You were right—maybe I'm not ready for stilts after all."

She couldn't help but wish that he were here now. He would know what to do. Why, she would even have been glad to see Mae Ella. "It's useless," she admitted finally. "I'd better be getting back."

Cr-a-a-a-c-k! A loud noise rose up in the woods. "What was that?" she cried. Willie Pearl leapt to her feet. She felt her heart try to escape from her chest. Again—the terrible sound. It made her insides twist and turn. Willie Pearl grabbed the lamp and took off running. So quick was she to leave that she forgot all about her precious stilt still leaning against the old log.

The terrible sound seemed to follow her as she ran. It matched the sound of her own breathing. Through the grove and down the slope toward old lady Chinkapin's she fled—or so she thought.

"Just a little ways more, and I should be in the clear," she figured, running hard. But in her fright, Willie Pearl did not realize that she was running the wrong way. What should have been the path just behind the familiar house instead seemed strange and foreboding.

She stepped out onto the mysterious path. In the next moment, Willie Pearl felt the soft earth beneath her give way. Firm ground now became a great empty space filled only with dead leaves, broken branches, loose dirt, falling rock, and finally, darkness.

Chapter 7

It was the sharp pain of her left ankle throbbing that caused Willie Pearl to come to. Only then did she start to notice the wooziness in her head and how sore the rest of her felt.

"Uh-h-h-h, what's happened to me? Where am I?" she moaned.

Willie Pearl opened her eyes wide and strained to see around her. But the perfect darkness gave her no clues. Even on nights when there was no moon at all, Willie Pearl could still see a little in the darkness—the faint outline of the bedpost, or the edges of the door frame in her room. But here, it was impossible to see her own hand not six inches in front of her face.

Groggy and confused, she said, "I've got to get up, or I'll be late for school." Willie Pearl tried to stand. The pain from her ankle overwhelmed her, and she dropped back down to where she had fallen.

Some time later, Willie Pearl woke again. The aching and the darkness were as intense as before. But this time, it was the smells she noticed first. There was no "good morning" scent of breakfast meat frying or coffee on the brew—not even the warm, smoky scent from the fireplace in the front room. Instead, the smells that met her nose were musty and strong. They reminded her of Papa's dirty muckers when he first came home from work or the coal stove on days when Johnny emptied the ashes.

Willie Pearl: Under the Mountain

"Ma, Papa—somebody help!" Her faint voice was swallowed up by the darkness. No answer came.

Unable to see, Willie Pearl began to feel around with her hands. Everything felt rough, and sharp, and cold. Suddenly, her fingers touched something that was different from the rest. Smooth metal . . . rounded glass . . . a thin handle. Willie Pearl's fingertips sent signals that her eyes could not see.

"It's a lamp!" she cried, relieved to find anything that she could recognize, at last. Carefully, she lifted it to her ear and gave it a shake. The sloshing noise let her know that it was still full of kerosene.

"A match . . . if only I had a match, I could see where I am," she said. With great difficulty, Willie Pearl propped herself up to a sitting position and began to search one pocket of her coat. Nothing there, she tried again. This time, her efforts were rewarded. Inside her right-hand pocket was not just one match, but a partially filled box of matchsticks. Ordinarily, Willie Pearl had no need of matches, and she certainly was not in the habit of carrying them around in her coat.

"This is strange," she thought to herself. "What are these doing in here?" She felt a lot like Alice when she first popped into Wonderland—mysterious and out of place. Willie Pearl did not wait to figure things out. Immediately, she struck the match. Its dim light was enough for her to see how to light the lamp. As she was taught, she snapped the used matchstick between her two fingers to make sure the match was out before she dropped it to the ground.

Willie Pearl held the lamp out at arm's length and surveyed her surroundings. All around her on the floor were mounds of rubble, bits of branches, and large chunks of rock. She stretched the lamp up as high up as her aching shoulder would allow.

Chapter 7

Large wooden posts spaced several feet apart stood like soldiers in a row. But the ones nearest her were not standing straight at all. The hefty wooden beams were bent at unnatural angles. They seemed to have been broken under some enormous weight. It was as if someone had snapped them in two like used matchsticks.

"Snapped in two like matchsticks . . . ." Willie Pearl repeated her thoughts out loud as if she had heard the phrase before. "Snapped in two like matchsticks!" Then, she remembered. "Mr. Jack! At the supper table, Mr. Jack said that when they went into the mine, there was rock fall, and the timbers were snapped in two like matchsticks!" Willie Pearl sucked in her breath quickly in horror. "That's it—I must have fallen into the mine when I went looking for Johnny's knife! I'm somewhere under the mountain!"

Willie Pearl had known fear before, but nothing could compare with the few moments that followed. She felt all things at once—her heart pounding, her blood rushing, her lungs pumping, her skin tingling, her eyes popping, her ears ringing, her throat closing. The more she thought about her impossible situation, the more terrified she became. And while the truth was horrible enough, her own imagination made it even worse.

Willie Pearl thought back to the conversation around the supper table. Papa had said that there was rock fall. That meant that the roof of the mine must be caving in. "It could happen at any moment," she thought. "I could be crushed!"

Mr. Jack had said that last spring, Andy couldn't get out in time. "That means I might never see Ma or Papa or Johnny or anyone ever again," she cried. The dreadful thoughts kept coming.

Papa said that the coal company had shut down the mine until the safety inspectors came. "I'm here all alone," she realized. "No one will even be looking for me!" And then, the most terrifying of all thoughts came.

Mr. Lucias wanted to know what would happen if the inspectors found out that the men had been mining too close to the surface. "That's when they'll blast that part of the tunnel shut," she remembered.

"It's hopeless. If only I had listened to Papa. I should have just told Johnny the truth about his knife. It's lost forever. And now, I'll never have the chance to say, 'I'm sorry.'" There was no way that Willie Pearl could keep back the rush of tears any longer. Her wails echoed back from the walls of coal and rock. Lost in its midst, there was no comfort to be found in her beloved mountain.

Chapter 8

There was no such thing as a day off in a coal mining town. Even though the mine had been shut down, the men were up and at the breakfast table by four o'clock, as usual.

"I've been itching to do some rabbit hunting," exclaimed Mr. Jack. "Why, I'll be back with a whole sackful in time for you to skin 'em for dinner," he bragged to Ma Rainey. "Care to join me, Lucias?"

"Thanks just the same, but I've already been nabbed to help with some chores around here," said Mr. Lucias.

"Don't blame that on me," Papa said, blowing the steam from his coffee. "Put that on Rainey. She's the one."

"No sense wasting these good pork chops on a bunch of lazybones," Ma pretended to fuss. "I've fed you good, now let's see what kind of work I can get out of you."

"Well, I guess I'll be taking off right about now," said Mr. Jack. "Rabbits in the woods can't wait."

It was more than two hours later when Johnny, Susie Mae, and Clint came down to breakfast. Willie Pearl was not there, but then, there was nothing normal about this day. The children couldn't remember when Papa had been home during a school day, unless he was having a sick spell. He and Mr. Lucias were busy breaking up a patch of the hillside so that Ma could put in a bigger vegetable garden.

With all of the unusual activity going on, everybody figured that Willie Pearl was around somewhere with someone else. But by the time breakfast was over, it was clear that Willie

Pearl had not been seen that morning by anyone. It was not long until the truth came to light.

Mr. Jack came banging in the front door with a start. "Mahone, Lucias . . ." he yelled, "you'd better come hear this!" Papa, Lucias, Ma Rainey, and the three children came running.

"I was hunting rabbit up in the woods when the darndest thing happened." Mr. Jack was out of breath. He had run all the way back to the house. "There was this rabbit, you see, the fattest one I had spotted all morning," Mr. Jack continued. "No sooner did I get him in my sights than he took off running. I must have chased him halfway through the woods."

"You called us in to tell us that?" questioned Papa.

"No, no, listen," insisted Mr. Jack. "I ended up right around old lady Chinkapin's house, you know, back of the holler?"

"Yes," said Papa, "go on."

"Well, I didn't believe it myself at first, but there, right out in plain daylight, was this big crack. The ground was split open like a ripe melon!"

"What do you mean?" asked Mr. Lucias. "I don't follow you."

"I'm talking about a mine break. I told you we didn't need any big shots to tell us anything. We're tunneling out in back of old lady Chinkapin's place. You need to come take a look!"

"That's mighty dangerous news, alright," agreed Papa. "We'd better go down to the mine office right away. If that's so, they won't need to wait until the safety inspector gets here. They might want to dynamite the area off altogether so it won't get any worse." The three men headed for the front door.

"Wait a minute, Mr. Jack," interrupted Ma Rainey. "Before you leave, by any chance did Willie Pearl sneak off with you to do some rabbit hunting? We haven't seen her all morning."

"No, ma'am," said Mr. Jack. "Rabbit hunting is no place for

girls, not even for a tomboy like Butch."

"What's that you're carrying, Mr. Jack?" Susie Mae asked. For the first time, everyone noticed a large wooden pole.

"I found this not far from the break. I used it to poke around a little, to see if I could tell how deep it was. But the break is deeper than this old stick could measure." He twirled it around. What the others had missed, Johnny recognized immediately.

"That's Willie Pearl's!" he blurted out. "That's her stilt! Look—her initials are even carved at the bottom!" There, etched in the wood, were the initials "W.P."

"So that's what you two have been working on in secret," nodded Ma Rainey.

"No, you don't understand. I hid her stilts under the house for her on Saturday, and they were still there last night. If Mr. Jack found one up there this morning, then that means . . . ." Here Johnny stopped.

"Means what?" asked Susie Mae, innocently.

"That Willie Pearl must have been messing around up in those woods against my orders," shouted Papa. "Johnny, Jack, you go searching for her up in the woods. Lucias, come with me. We've got to get down to the mine office right away!"

Down below, Willie Pearl had no way of knowing whether it was day or night, or even how long she had been under the mountain. But, there was one thing she did know. If there was any chance of escape, it would depend on her, and her alone.

Hoisting the lamp up once again, Willie Pearl strained to see in the dark. She circled the lamp around slowly, taking in every detail of the gloomy chamber. Jagged black walls layered with coal and rock, trickles of water that ran down the walls, wooden timbers as big around as Willie Pearl herself, and, at the foot of the timbers—steel railroad tracks! She had not noticed them before. But, there they were, spaced evenly along the floor of the mine. The tracks stretched as far as her light would show.

Willie Pearl tried to remember everything Papa had taught her about the mine. When the men blasted the coal from the walls of the mountain, they loaded it up in coal cars. The cars ran in and out of the mine, just like a railroad.

"If I just follow the tracks, sooner or later, they'll lead me to the outside." That thought gave Willie Pearl her first bit of hope. But that hope was dashed as quickly as it had come. "Papa said that these tunnels twist and turn every which a way. I could stumble around inside here for days," she realized. "I might never make it out at all!"

Willie Pearl shivered, then pulled her coat to her. The cold, dark, dampness of the mine blanketed her entirely. One by one, she saw the faces of those she loved, above the mountain— Papa, Ma Rainey, Susie Mae, Clint, Johnny. The loneliness was worse than the cold.

"How foolish to have been afraid of something as silly as walking on stilts," she thought. In that moment, the gentle words of her brother that day returned to her in the darkness.

"You can't just stand still. You gotta move to keep from falling," he had said. "Remember, it all depends on you. Just put one foot in front of the other until you're through." In those words was everything she needed.

Slowly, painfully, Willie Pearl rose to her feet and took the first step. The lamp shone ahead of her only a few feet. It struck the metal rails dimly, allowing her to take one or two steps at a time. She stooped down low to see the rails better, and to ease the aching of her hurt ankle. Step after determined step, Willie Pearl edged on in the darkness.

Chapter 8

"You can't just stand still.
You gotta move to keep from falling."

At every bend and turn, Willie Pearl did not know whether she was going forward, or deeper in the mine. "Should I go right, or left?" she wondered. Whatever choice she made, Willie Pearl did not stand still. On she pressed, for minutes, or hours, she could not tell.

Papa, Mr. Lucias, and the foreman gathered at the entrance of the mine. In the broad daylight, the three men poured over a map. It showed every chamber and tunnel in the mine.

"There's no point upsetting everybody until we know what's what," the foreman insisted. "We'll go in and have a look around, first. I'll take the main line. Lucias, you take the east section. Mahone, you go west."

The three men stood with their backs to the mine entrance. Had they turned around sooner, they might have noticed a faint beam of light inching along toward the mine's opening. Out of the darkness, a small voice called out.

"Papa, I'm here!" the voice said, barely above a whisper.

Papa wheeled around suddenly. "Willie Pearl? Is that you? Quick, shine a light. I think I heard her," he yelled.

Papa did not wait for the others. He turned and ran straight toward the pinpoint of light that shone out from the empty cave. Running into the mine, he reached his daughter just in time to scoop her up from the ground where she crumpled.

"It's her, it's really her! It's my Willie Pearl! Thank the good Lord, she's safe!" Papa drew his daughter to his chest in a tight but loving grip. Over and over, he kissed her dirty, tear-streaked face.

Mr. Lucias, excited and relieved, offered to help Papa carry her limp body back up to the house where the others would be waiting. But Papa would not let her go. Willie Pearl did not leave his arms until he rested her gently, safely back in her own room.

45

Chapter 9

"Here, try another spoonful of this," said Susie Mae as she offered her sister the steaming bowl.

Even Ma Rainey's best chicken soup could not cover up the horrible taste of the Syrup of Black Draught. Ma Rainey had been making Willie Pearl take it for days. The thick, dark medicine coated Willie Pearl's tongue and stained her teeth with its awful blackness. It reminded her of the roofing tar Papa and Mr. Jack had used to stick the tarpaper roof on with a few weeks ago. Not even the penny candy that Mae Ella brought by could get the taste out of her mouth completely.

"How much longer you have to wear that thing anyway?" asked Susie Mae. She wrinkled up her nose and pointed to a pouch strung around Willie Pearl's neck.

"Ma says a few more days . . . just to make sure." Willie Pearl fanned her nose with her hand.

The asifedita bag was filled with strong-smelling herbs intended to keep colds, croup, headaches, fever, and other miseries away. It must be some kind of powerful stuff, thought Willie Pearl, as she fingered the homemade cotton bag. She remembered Papa had worn one for three whole weeks when he had his sick spell last year.

Johnny and Clint had taken to sleeping on quilts downstairs in the front room while Willie Pearl healed up. Even though Willie Pearl liked not having to yank the covers from her sister Susie all night, she would still be glad when the boys moved back in. She missed whispering back and forth through the makeshift curtain that separated the boys' bed from theirs. She even missed Susie Mae's cold feet on the backs of her legs in the night.

Susie Mae was turning out to be an excellent nursemaid. She attended to her sister day and night—bringing her fresh rags to wrap her swollen ankle, cleaning her cuts and scrapes, even consoling her after the switching she had gotten for disobeying Papa's orders.

Johnny had not gone unpunished either. "You're old enough to know better," Papa had said sternly. "You should have told me about that mine break as soon as you spotted it. Thank the good Lord—things could have been a lot worse." Ma suggested that Johnny would have plenty of time to think about the error of his ways while taking over *all* of Willie Pearl's chores.

As to the knife, it turned out that Johnny had it all the time! "You should have come to me," said Johnny. "I picked it up from the log before we left that day. It was never missing at all!"

Susie Mae handed her sister a napkin. "Willie . . . there's something I've been meaning to ask you." Susie's face turned suddenly serious. She poked at first a carrot, then a turnip beneath the chicken broth with the spoon. "How did it feel being stuck down there, you know, all alone?"

Willie Pearl drew the quilt up around her shoulders and hugged her knees to her chest real tight. The late afternoon sunlight peered in through the half-open window shade, and the walls took on a pinkish color. Even though the tiny room was quite cozy, made warm by the coal stove in the kitchen below, Willie Pearl shivered a bit.

"I was awful scared," Willie Pearl began, "more scared than ever before. I thought I would never see you or Johnny or anybody ever again." Willie Pearl's eyes grew large and teary.

"C'mon, just one more sip, and you'll be done."

"What made you . . . try?" said Susie Mae, scooting next to her on the bed. Susie put one arm around her little sister and stroked her long braids.

Willie Pearl waited a long while before answering. She gazed out the window and saw the mountain rising straight up to the sky. The fast-setting sun was barely peeking above it now. Watching it, she remembered the darkness, the cold, and how alone she had felt under the mountain.

"Something made me try," Willie Pearl began again. "Even when I felt like giving up, something made me try. I kept telling myself 'just put one foot in front of the other.' It was kinda like learning to walk on stilts—you just have to put one foot in front of the other until you're through, even when you're scared."

Susie Mae thought back to how afraid she had been when the Jackson's house caught fire last year. Everyone in the holler—young and old—had pitched in to help put the fire out. It seemed that all the water in Number 6 holler would not be enough to stop the angry flames. But the house was saved, one bucket at a time.

"I guess it's that same way no matter what you do," Susie Mae said thoughtfully. "Sometimes you just have to find a way, no matter how you feel inside."

The two girls sat quietly for a moment in the darkening room. All at once, Susie Mae leaned over and tickled the underside of Willie Pearl's nose with the end of her braid. Their laughter broke the silence and filled the corners of the room.

"You're gonna be just fine," said Susie Mae, reaching for the bowl of soup. "You'll be back on those stilts in no time." She raised the spoon once more to Willie Pearl's lips. "C'mon, just one more sip," she said, "and you'll be done."

About the Author

Michelle Y. Green is the daughter of Willie Pearl Mahone and Eddie Lee Young, of Number 6 and 5 hollers, Jenkins, Kentucky. A graduate of the University of Maryland with a B.S. in Journalism, Michelle, with her husband, Oliver, is a principal of The Greentree Group, Inc.—a writing/editorial/ design firm in Temple Hills, Maryland. Their son, 7-year-old Bryan, is an avid reader and likes to create books of his own. The Green family anxiously anticipates the birth of their second child this fall.

About the Illustrator

Steve McCracken lives and works in Washington, D.C. His work appears regularly in magazines and newspapers throughout the country, including *The Washington Post*. Steve is married and has two teenaged children. Steve's illustrations for *Willie Pearl* won the prestigious Edpress *Excellence in Print Award* for "Best Illustrations."

About Willie Pearl

Willie Pearl Mahone left the mountains of Kentucky in 1944 and married Eddie Lee Young, one of the first triple-rated black pilots in the Army-Air Corps. Pearl has traveled extensively, yet always finds time to return to Number 6 to visit Jessie Mae, Susie Mae, and Johnny several times a year. Little brother Clint, now in Ohio, comes down often. Pearl lives in southern Maryland where she divides her time among her three daughters—Marie, Michelle, and Adrienne—and three grandchildren—Shannon, Bryan, and Brandon. She looks forward to the arrival of her new grandchild this fall.